CATCHING THE VELOCIRAPTOR

DINOSAUR COVE™

CATCHING THE
VELOCIRAPTOR

BY
REX STONE

ILLUSTRATED BY
MIKE SPOOR

LITTLE APPLE

SCHOLASTIC INC.

New York Toronto London Auckland Sydney
Mexico City New Delhi Hong Kong Buenos Aires

SPECIAL THANKS TO JANE CLARKE

FOR GUY MACDONALD,
A TRUE EXPLORER OF ADVENTURES

No part of this publication may be reproduced, stored in a retrieval system, or transmitted in any form or by any means, electronic, mechanical, photocopying, recording, or otherwise, without written permission of the publisher. For information regarding permission, write to Working Partners Ltd., Stanley House, St. Chad's Place, London WC1X 9HH, United Kingdom.

ISBN-13: 978-0-545-05381-5
ISBN-10: 0-545-05381-1

Dinosaur Cove series created by Working Partners Ltd., London.

Published by Scholastic Inc., 557 Broadway,
New York, NY 10012, by arrangement with Working Partners Ltd.
SCHOLASTIC, LITTLE APPLE, and associated logos are trademarks
and/or registered trademarks of Scholastic Inc. DINOSAUR COVE is
a registered trademark of Working Partners Ltd.

12 11 10 9 8 7 6 5 4 3 2 1   9 10 11 12 13 14/0

Printed in China
First printing, February 2009

FACT FILE

➡ JAMIE HAS JUST MOVED FROM THE CITY TO LIVE IN THE LIGHTHOUSE IN DINOSAUR COVE. JAMIE'S DAD IS OPENING A DINOSAUR MUSEUM ON THE BOTTOM FLOOR OF THE LIGHTHOUSE. WHEN JAMIE GOES HUNTING FOR FOSSILS IN THE CRUMBLING CLIFFS ON THE BEACH HE MEETS A LOCAL BOY, TOM, AND THE TWO DISCOVER AN AMAZING SECRET: A WORLD WITH REAL, LIVE DINOSAURS! THE BOYS HAVE EXPLORED THE JUNGLE, THE MARSH, AND THE CLIFFS, BUT WHEN THEY SPEND TIME AT THE LAGOON, THEY END UP FISHING FOR TROUBLE!

JAMIE

- FULL NAME: JAMIE MORGAN
- AGE: 8 YEARS
- SIZE: 1 JATOM*
- TOP SPEED: 7 MPH
- LIKES: FOSSIL HUNTING AND LEARNING ABOUT DINOSAURS
- DISLIKES: BEING STUCK INDOORS

Jamie's eye

Jamie's foot

Jamie's hand

*NOTE: A JATOM IS THE SIZE OF JAMIE OR TOM: 4 FT TALL AND 60 LB IN WEIGHT.

TOM

- FULL NAME: THOMAS CLAY
- AGE: 8 YEARS
- SIZE: 1 JATOM*
- TOP SPEED: 7 MPH
- LIKES: TRACKING ANIMALS AND EXPLORING WILDLIFE
- DISLIKES: RAINY DAYS

Tom's eye Tom's Hand

WANNA

- FULL NAME: WANNANOSAURUS
- AGE: 65 – 80 MILLION YEARS**
- SIZE: LESS THAN A JATOM*
- TOP SPEED: 31 MPH, ESPECIALLY WHEN BEING CHASED BY A T-REX
- LIKES: STINKY GINKGO FRUIT AND BANGING HIS HEAD ON TREE TRUNKS
- DISLIKES: SCARY DINOSAURS

Wanna's head Wanna's foot

*NOTE: A JATOM IS THE SIZE OF JAMIE OR TOM: 4 FT TALL AND 60 LB IN WEIGHT.
**NOTE: SCIENTISTS CALL THIS PERIOD THE LATE CRETACEOUS.

VELOCIRAPTOR

Velociraptor's claw

Velociraptor's eye

Velociraptor's teeth

Velociraptor's tail

- FULL NAME: VELOCIRAPTOR
- AGE: 65 – 85 MILLION YEARS**
- HEIGHT: LESS THAN ONE JATOM*
- LENGTH: 1 1/2 JATOMS*
- WEIGHT: 1 JATOM*
- TOP SPEED: 35 MPH
- LIKES: PLAYING WITH HIS FOOD AND STEALING SHINY OBJECTS
- DISLIKES: THINGS THAT GET AWAY

*NOTE: A JATOM IS THE SIZE OF JAMIE OR TOM: 4 FT TALL AND 60 LB IN WEIGHT.
**NOTE: SCIENTISTS CALL THIS PERIOD THE LATE CRETACEOUS.

Landslips where clay and fossils are

Muddy beach

DINO CAVE

High tide beach line

—Low tide beach line

Sea

Smugglers' Point

CHAPTER 1

SEARCH.

ABCDEFGHIJKLMN
OPQRSTUVWXYZ

Jamie Morgan pulled a rainbow-colored metal fish out of his grandfather's tackle box and held it up for his friend, Tom Clay, to see. "This fish has feathers!" A cluster of tiny pink and orange feathers sprouted out from where the tail should be.

"Different baits catch different beasts," Jamie's grandfather said with a grin, holding out his hand for the feathery fish. "This spinner is great for catching sea bass. Now, let's see. What else will I need today?"

sea bass spinner

crab line

He tipped a tangle of weights, spinners, and fishing line onto the kitchen floor of the old lighthouse.

"What's this?" Jamie picked up an H-shaped piece of orange plastic with string wrapped around it and a couple of heavy lead weights dangling from it.

"Haven't you seen one before?" Tom said in amazement. "It's a crab line."

Jamie shook his head. "How can this catch crabs?"

"It's easy," Tom said. "You tie a bit of bacon rind on the end and throw it in. The crabs grab the bacon and you grab the crabs!"

"Cool!" said Jamie. "I'd like to try that."

"The best place for crabbing is Sealight Head at high tide," Jamie's grandfather said, as he crammed everything but the crab line back in his tackle box. "But high tide isn't until later this afternoon. I'll meet you there, if you like, after I've caught some sea bass for dinner."

"OK, Grandpa," Jamie said as the old man finished packing his tackle box. "We'll wait until then."

"We don't have to wait," Tom whispered to Jamie. "We could go crabbing in Misty Lagoon in Dino World right now."

Dino World was Jamie and Tom's secret — even Jamie's grandfather didn't know that they'd found a world where real live dinosaurs lived.

"Great idea!" Jamie winked at Tom. "We'll meet you near Sealight Head later, Grandpa."

"Don't forget the bait and mop bucket to put the crabs in," Jamie's grandfather told them. He pulled on his fishing boots. "And I've put two cheese and pickle sandwiches in the fridge for you."

He headed for the door. "Have fun!"

"We will," Tom said with a smile. The minute Jamie's grandfather was out the door, Tom grabbed the handle of the mop bucket. "Got your Fossil Finder, Jamie?"

"Already in my backpack." Jamie grinned as he wrapped two cheese and pickle sandwiches in shiny aluminum foil and made a separate package for the bacon. He stuffed them in his backpack along with the crab line. "Let's go!"

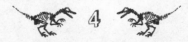

The boys clattered down
the stairs of the lighthouse and
dashed through the dinosaur
exhibits on the ground floor.
Jamie's dad was busy fixing a
label to the wall next to the
triceratops skull.

"How's the museum going,
Mr. Morgan?" Tom asked.

"Great, thanks," said Jamie's
dad. "The Grand Opening is
only a few days away."

"See ya, Dad!" Jamie called, hurrying past the Late Cretaceous model and the T-Rex display. "We're going crabbing."

The boys scrambled down the rocky path from the lighthouse and ran along the beach onto the trail that led up Smugglers' Point. They stopped to catch their breath, and then clambered up the boulders to the smugglers' cave and squeezed through the gap at the back into the secret chamber.

"This is my favorite place in the whole world!" Jamie's heart began to pound as soon as he placed his feet into the fossilized dinosaur footprints on the cave floor.

"One . . . two . . . three . . ." He counted each step. "Keep close behind me, Tom."

"You bet." Tom's voice sounded excited. "I wonder what we're going to find this time."

"Four . . ."

A crack of light appeared in the cave wall in front of him.

"Five!" The ground squelched beneath Jamie's feet and he stood blinking in the bright sunshine and breathing in the familiar warm wet-leaf smell of Dino World.

 7

CHAPTER 2

A second later, Jamie and Tom were standing on Ginkgo Hill, and a rough, slobbery tongue was licking Jamie's hand.

"Ready for another adventure, Wanna?" Jamie asked their little dinosaur friend.

Jamie picked a stinky ginkgo fruit and held it out to the wannanosaurus.

Wanna took it gently, then greedily gobbled it up, wagging his tail and grunting as smelly ginkgo juice dribbled down his chin.

"It's almost like he was waiting for us," Tom said with a laugh.

With Tom and Wanna close behind, Jamie strode through the trees to a curtain of vines at the edge of Ginkgo Hill. As he pushed the vines aside, excitement fizzed like soda in his stomach.

Beneath them lay the steamy emerald-green jungle. The air throbbed with the whirring and buzzing of insects, and the jungle rang with the strange calls of the weird and wonderful creatures that only lived in Dino World.

"This has got to be the best place for adventures in the whole wide world!" Jamie announced with a huge grin on his face.

"In the whole solar system!" Tom cheered.

"In the whole universe!" Jamie exclaimed.

Wanna grunted his agreement.

"Come on!" Jamie said. "Let's see what we can catch in Misty Lagoon. We've only got until the tide comes in."

The three friends clambered down the steep hillside into the dense jungle.

"We can follow the stream," Jamie said, jumping into the shallow water that trickled and gurgled its way to the lagoon.

They splashed along the stream bed.

"That's where we met the T-Rex," Tom said, pointing to a jumble of huge rounded rocks.

"I'll never forget those teeth." Jamie shuddered. "I hope he's not around today."

"Me, too," said Tom, looking around nervously. "Let's go."

They ran until they burst out of the jungle and onto the palm-fringed sandy beach of the sparkling blue lagoon.

Jamie shaded his eyes with his hand and gazed around the shore. "Which would be the best spot to find prehistoric crabs?"

"We need deep water for crabbing," Tom told him. "It's no use wading into the shallows."

"How about over there?" Jamie pointed to an outcrop of fern-covered rocks on the northeast shore. A stone ledge stuck out of the ferns like a wide diving board, hanging over the deep, blue water.

"Perfect!" Tom declared.

Jamie led the way around the lagoon to the rocks and scrambled over them, pushing aside the plants. It was an easy climb to

the ledge over the water, and he put down his backpack in the shade of the tall ferns.

Tom scrambled up onto the ledge next to him. "We can't see much through these ferns," he said, glancing over his shoulder. "But Wanna will warn us if anything tries to sneak up."

He leaned over the lagoon and filled up the bucket with water. "Time to bait the line."

Jamie knelt on the rock ledge and dug inside his backpack.

"Here's the bacon." Jamie handed Tom the packet and then unraveled the crab line.

Wanna watched curiously as Tom unwrapped the bacon.

"No, Wanna, it's not for you," Tom told the little dinosaur, tearing off the bacon rind. Wanna leaned over Tom's shoulder. His long tongue shot toward the bacon.

Gak gak gak!

Wanna spluttered in disgust. He spun around and grabbed a mouthful of fern leaves.

"He's trying to get rid of the taste," Jamie said, tying the bacon rind onto the end of the line. "Plant eaters don't eat bacon."

Tom showed Jamie how to hold the orange plastic handle and carefully lower the crab line into the lagoon. Jamie felt the string run through his fingers until the weight came to rest on the bottom.

"Do I pull it up right away?" he asked.

"No." Tom laughed. "You have to be patient. You'll feel a tug on the line when something takes the bait."

"What if it isn't a crab?" Jamie asked. "What if it's a huge electric eel?"

"Ooh," Tom said. "What if it's a humongous stingray?"

"What if it's a Loch Ness monster with ginormous fangs?" As Jamie laughed, a big bubble broke the mirror surface of the water.

Pop!

Jamie leaped to his feet, startling Wanna, who nearly fell backward over the bucket.

But there was no giant creature leaping out at them. The lagoon was a calm mirror once more.

"False alarm," Tom said. "There's nothing there."

Wanna started to chew a fern stem.

"Wanna's got the right idea," Jamie said. "Let's have lunch while we wait."

"Good idea." Tom rummaged in the backpack and pulled out the packet of sandwiches. He unwrapped one and handed it to Jamie.

"Your grandpa's pickles are great!" Tom mumbled with his mouth full. "Even if they are a bit spicy," he said between coughs.

"Grandpa sure likes to make them hot," Jamie agreed, taking a huge bite. He felt a tug on the crab line. "Something's taken the bait!" he spluttered, spraying a mouthful of crumbs all over the rock. He threw down his sandwich and started to pull up the line as fast

 18

as he could. The line
went limp.

Tom and Jamie peered
over the ledge. "It got
away," Jamie realized
as the end of the
empty line came out of
the water. "It ate the
bacon, too."

"Better luck
next time." Tom
tore off another
strip of bacon and
attached it to the
dripping line. Jamie threw
it back in the water and reached
for his sandwich.

"Where's my sandwich?" he said. There
was a rustle in the ferns. Jamie whirled around
in time to see the ferns stirring as a creature
scurried away through them.

"Wanna!" Jamie yelled. "You sandwich thief!"

Jamie gave the handle of the crab line to Tom and hopped off the rock into the ferns. He could hear a strange high-pitched rattling noise.

Ack *ack* *ack!*

"Wanna?" he called. "Is that you?"

The ferns parted. The little dinosaur was bobbing his head and hopping excitedly from foot to foot. His tongue was hanging out and he was making strange noises.

Jamie knew what that meant: Wanna must have been spluttering on his grandfather's pickle. "It's your own fault. You shouldn't have stolen my sandwich," Jamie scolded him.

"Come quick!" Tom shouted from behind him. "We've caught something

big!"

CHAPTER 3

One, two, three. . . heave!"

Jamie and Tom pulled on the crab line with all their might.

"Look at the size of that!" Tom gasped.

Dangling from the crab line was the biggest crab that Jamie had ever seen. Its shell was the size of a dinner plate. The crab's silvery shell shone in the sunshine as it held tight to the bacon on the end of the line. As Tom held the line, Jamie grabbed the bucket.

Wanna edged up and sniffed at the crab. It waved a pincer at him.

Grunk!

Wanna jumped back in alarm as Tom lowered the crab gently into the bucket.

"It's a good thing this is a big bucket." Jamie laughed.

They peered inside. The crab was using its pincers to tear off small pieces of the bacon and shovel them into its mouth.

"Crabs haven't changed much since dino times," Tom said thoughtfully.

Jamie took out his Fossil Finder and flipped it open. The *HAPPY HUNTING* screen popped up and he typed *CRAB* into the search box. *CRABS*

CRAB

HAVEN'T CHANGED MUCH SINCE DINOSAUR TIMES, he read aloud.

Tom laughed. "That's what I said."

Jamie snapped the Fossil Finder shut and put it on the rock beside him. "I want to take a close look at this dino crab," he told Tom. "Help me get it off the line. It's wedged in the bucket, so it shouldn't nip us."

Tom held the bucket steady and Jamie untangled the line from the crab's pincers.

Just when he had finished, there was a sudden rustle in the ferns behind them.

Ack ^ack^ *ack!*

Jamie spun around to see what was making the noise. A turkey-sized dinosaur with open toothy jaws dashed out from the plants onto the ledge beside them.

26

Tom almost dropped the bucket in surprise.

Snap!

The new dinosaur grabbed the Fossil Finder
in its needle-sharp fangs.

Ack *ack ack ack ack!*

With a whip of the feathers on
the end of its long yellow and
orange tail, the two-legged
dinosaur turned and
darted into the ferns.

SNap!

"What was that?" Tom said, still holding the bucket.

"Th-that . . ." stammered Jamie, feeling the blood drain from his face, "that was a velociraptor. A velociraptor just stole my Fossil Finder!"

Tom looked startled.

"We have to get it back," Jamie said, shoving the crab line into his backpack.

Jamie crashed into the tall ferns and raced after the rapidly retreating raptor. Tom and Wanna plunged after him.

"It's heading toward the Far Away Mountains," Tom said as they emerged from the ferns into a section of the plains they hadn't been to before.

"Why did you bring the crab?" Jamie asked as they puffed along a shallow stream that flowed down to the lagoon.

Tom looked down in amazement at the

bucket that swung from his hand. "Forgot I had it," he said. "I'll take it back later."

Ahead of them, the velociraptor darted into a narrow passageway where the stream gushed between two huge rocks.

"Careful," Tom said. "We don't know what's on the other side of the rocks."

"Time to find out." Jamie stepped into the cool, fast-moving stream. Edging sideways, he squeezed through the narrow gap, followed closely by Tom and Wanna.

"Wow," he breathed. "It's like a rainbow!"

Ahead, the stream flowed through a rocky area streaked with splashes of bright orange, yellow, and green mud and cratered with deep blue pools that sparkled in the sunshine.

"There's the raptor!" Tom pointed to a reptilian tail disappearing into a cave on the other side of the pools.

"That must be where it lives." Jamie heaved a sigh of relief. "Urgh!" he sputtered. "It stinks like rotten eggs around here."

"Wanna likes it," Tom said, glancing at the little dinosaur. Wanna was standing next to one of the small pools with his snout in the air, sniffing deeply.

"He would," Jamie laughed. "He likes anything stinky."

Wanna cocked his head to one side and peered into the pool.

"Is he looking for more crabs?"

As Tom spoke, Wanna's pool burbled and bubbled. *Pop!* A wisp of hot steam escaped from a burst bubble and the smell of rotten eggs welled up.

"The water's hot." Jamie chuckled. "The only crabs he'll find in there will be bright red cooked ones."

Suddenly, there was a great

whoosh!

Wanna leaped back from the pool as a column of steaming water gushed high into the air.

Jamie watched it, mesmerized.

"Get out of the way!" Tom yelled as the column collapsed and a torrent of scalding water fell toward them.

CHAPTER 4

Jamie, Tom, and Wanna dived behind a rock as scalding drops of water rained down.

"It's a geyser," Tom said excitedly. "I saw one on a TV show about Yellowstone Park. The water's heated by melted rock that bubbles up from the center of the earth."

The boys and Wanna peered out from behind the rock. On the other side of the pools, near the raptor's cave, there was a hissing and popping and another geyser whooshed and spurted into the air. Each of the six pools took

their turn to shoot jets of hot water and steam into the air.

"No wonder that velociraptor's chosen to live in this cave," murmured Tom. "What other dinosaur would be fast enough to run past all the boiling geysers?"

"If we're careful, we can do it," Jamie said. "We've got to get the Fossil Finder back. If we leave it behind here, it might get fossilized — then someone in the future could dig up a computer next to a dinosaur fossil. We'll just have to learn the geysers' pattern."

osh!

The boys watched as the geysers repeated their eruptions.

"I think I got it," Jamie said.

The valley had gone quiet again. The only sound was the stream. It was as if nothing had happened.

"Now!" Tom yelled, clutching the crab bucket to his chest.

The boys and Wanna sprinted past the first pool.

Whoosh!

The huge geyser shot into the air behind them.

Whoosh!

"Watch out!" Jamie shouted. The three jumped into the stream and hid under an overhanging rock as the hot rain pattered into the water. As soon as it had passed, Wanna darted out and dashed past the second pool and the third, dodging the bubbling water.

"Follow Wanna!" Jamie yelled to Tom, and they raced after their dinosaur friend as all around them steaming fountains of scalding water exploded from the mini-geysers.

Whoosh!

In front of the cave, an
aquamarine pool began to gurgle.

Whoosh!

"Geyser about to blow!" Tom shouted
above the sound of the fast-flowing
stream. Jamie, Tom, and Wanna
sprinted past the gurgling pool
and hurled themselves
behind a rock at the
edge of the cave
mouth as the last
geyser exploded
with a *whoosh!*

"That was close."

Tom caught his breath and then peered into the bucket. "The dino crab seems to be OK. It's waving its pincers, though. I think it's annoyed."

"I'm not surprised." Jamie grinned, glancing at his watch. "We have to hurry," he told Tom. "It'll be high tide soon. We've got to get back before Grandpa comes looking for us."

"Sshh!" Tom whispered. "Wanna can hear something."

Wanna was
peering into the
cave with his tail
sticking out stiffly
behind him.

Ack *ack* *ack* *ack* *ack!*

A high-pitched rattle came from the back
of the cave. Wanna shot backward, making
grunting noises.

"Hide!" Jamie hissed. The boys and Wanna
ducked back behind the rock but nothing came
out of the cave.

"We'll have to be careful," Tom whispered,
gently putting down the crab bucket. "That's
the raptor's den, and animals are dangerous if
you corner them in their den."

They peered into the cave. Against the wall, near the entrance, was a nest like a bird's, but woven from dried ferns, and the size of a car tire. The sun was sparkling on shiny objects set among the brown stalks and leaves.

"Velociraptors must collect shiny things, like magpies," Tom said. "I can see the Fossil Finder!"

Jamie breathed a sigh of relief. "It's really close and there's no sign of the raptor. He must have gone deeper into the cave. Maybe we can just grab the Fossil Finder and get out of here."

Tom nodded. "Let's try."

They quietly crept into the gloomy, dank cave and tiptoed toward the velociraptor's nest. Jamie's foot crunched on something. *Ugh!* He looked down and shuddered. Well-gnawed bones were scattered around the huge nest.

"It's like the nest of a giant bird of prey," Tom whispered from behind him. "If that raptor gets us, we're in big trouble."

A prickle of fear ran down Jamie's spine. He knew they had to be very careful.

Suddenly, the velociraptor shot out of the darkness, snarling viciously.

Ack ack ack ack ack!

CHAPTER 5

Jamie threw himself backward as the raptor pounced.

Snap!

The raptor's needle-sharp teeth closed on empty air.

"Get out, quick!" Tom grabbed Jamie by the T-shirt and pulled him out of the cave and back behind the rock, nearly knocking over the dino crab bucket in the process.

Once more, they peered around the rock with Wanna grunting softly behind them.

Ack ack ack ack ack!

The velociraptor was rattling softly to itself as it bent over its nest and carefully rearranged the position of the Fossil Finder, placing it right in the center. The whoosh of the geysers exploded down in the valley, drowning out all sound.

"If we lure it out of the cave," Jamie whispered to Tom, "then I can dash in and grab the Fossil Finder."

"We lured the
ankylosaurus out of the
mud with flowers," Tom
said. "But the velociraptor
is a carnivore."

Jamie glanced at the
crab in the bucket. "I've
got an idea!" He rummaged
in his backpack, took out
the crab line, and tied
on the remains of the
bacon.

"Cool!" Tom grinned,
taking the line. "I've never
crabbed for dinosaurs
before."

Tom scrambled up onto
the rocks above the cave
and lowered the crab
line so that the bacon

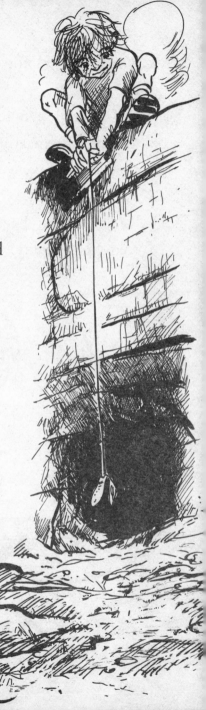

dangled at raptor height in the mouth of the cave.

The valley quieted again as Jamie and Wanna flattened themselves behind the rock at the side of the cave entrance. Wanna grunted softly to himself.

"We have to be patient for crabbing," Jamie told the little dinosaur.

Suddenly, the raptor lunged out of the mouth of the cave, reaching for the bacon with its sharp talons, but Tom jerked the crab line up and away. The raptor spread the feathers on its tail and forelimbs and launched itself into the air after the meat, but it was too high.

Tom lowered the bacon in front of the vicious dinosaur again, but pulled it away before it could grab it. The raptor leaped again and boxed at the bacon on the end of the line.

"It's like a kitten playing with a piece of string," Jamie whispered to Wanna.

Tom edged along the rock shelf above the mouth of the cave, taking the bacon bait farther and farther away from where Jamie and Wanna were hiding.

"It worked!" Jamie said. He darted into the cave and grabbed the Fossil Finder out of the nest. He was about to hurry away when he spotted the foil that had been wrapped around his sandwich — it had been the raptor that stole his sandwich, not Wanna!

I can't leave that to get fossilized, he thought, snatching it up. Jamie kept to the shadows and crept back the way he had come.

So far, so good, he thought, and he poked his head cautiously out of the cave.

Instead of seeing Wanna's friendly face, two cold reptilian eyes stared unblinkingly back at him.

"Oh, no!" Jamie breathed.

The velociraptor was back. It tilted its head to one side.

Ack ack ack!

The raptor rattled ominously and began to twitch its tail from side to side.

*Ack
  ack
    ack!*

Jamie's blood ran cold. It looked like a cat preparing to pounce on its prey.

"It's going to attack!" Tom screamed from the ledge above as the velociraptor spread its talon-like claws and came toward Jamie.

CHAPTER 6

Jamie was frozen to the spot. Any moment now, the raptor's sharp teeth and claws would tear him to pieces.

Something scratched at the ground behind him. Jamie whirled around. Wanna! Wanna was revving up, getting a claw hold on the rock, his bony head lowered . . .

Gaaaaak!

The little dinosaur charged just as the velociraptor sprang at Jamie.

Thwack!

Wanna barged into the velociraptor and bowled it over.

As the raptor spat and rattled furiously, struggling to get back to its feet, Jamie and Wanna raced behind the rock.

"Look out for the crab!" Jamie yelled. Too late. Wanna's tail smacked into the bucket and knocked it over. Jamie watched as the large dino crab tumbled out, pinched its claws at him, and scuttled away. It headed toward the stream, its silvery shell sparkling in the sunshine.

The stunned raptor stood up, shook itself, and looked around menacingly. Its tail feathers stiffened as it spotted the silvery crab scuttling past.

The raptor lunged after the crab. The crab darted this way and that as the raptor chased it.

56

"See! Raptors like shiny things!" Tom yelled from the ledge above the cave as the raptor turned, crouched, and sprang toward the crab.

Snap!

The raptor's teeth crunched together on thin air.

Dino Crab hasn't got a chance, Jamie thought, but then stared in amazement as the crab waved its pincers defiantly at the raptor, rushed toward it, and pinched it on the calf of its left leg.

Ack! The raptor leaped back in surprise and pain.

"Go, Dino Crab!" the boys cheered, as the crab scuttled away from the raptor, toward the tumbling cool stream. They watched it plop into the water and sail like a boat downstream toward Misty Lagoon.

The velociraptor raced after the crab, dodging spouts of hot steam as, one after another, the geysers erupted all around it.

"Dino Crab can take care of itself." Tom laughed. "That velociraptor has met its match!"

Jamie looked at his watch. "We better get back," he yelled up to Tom.

"I can see Ginkgo Hill from up here," Tom called down. "We can go across the plains."

"Great!" Jamie grabbed the bucket
and he and Wanna clambered up onto
the rock ledge above the cave. As they
climbed, the green top of Ginkgo Hill rose in
the distance. "I'm glad we don't have to go
back through the geysers."

Wanna greeted Tom with a wag of his tail,
then strode off along the narrow path that
led away from the cave. At the top, Jamie put
down the bucket and shaded his eyes to look

60

out across the gently rolling plains that lay
between them and Ginkgo Hill. On the edge
of the plains, a herd of small stocky dinosaurs
with big bony neck frills and parrot-like beaks
was grazing peacefully on the horsetail ferns.

Jamie rummaged in his backpack and
took out the Fossil Finder. Its shiny case was
dented with raptor tooth marks. He rubbed off
a streak of dried raptor drool and then flipped
it open.

"It still works," he said in relief as he typed in *NECK FRILL* and *BEAK*.

Tom looked over his shoulder. *PROTOCERATOPS*, he read. "They're harmless." He put the crab line in the bucket and picked it up. "And they wouldn't be browsing if any carnivores were around."

Wanna bobbed his head as if in agreement, turned, and set off toward Ginkgo Hill, followed by Tom. Jamie snapped the Fossil Finder shut, crammed it into his backpack, and hurried after them.

"He knows all the paths around here," Tom said, as Wanna confidently led them past the herd of peaceful protoceratops and through the jumbles of rock and tangles of tree ferns that littered the plains. They followed the little dinosaur across the stream and back up the conifer-carpeted hillside to the top of Ginkgo Hill.

Jamie checked his watch. "We should make it in time to meet Grandpa," he said, giving Wanna a pat on the head. "Bye, Wanna, see you next time. Sorry I accused you of stealing my sandwich."

Jamie picked a handful of ginkgo fruit and the little dinosaur grunted happily as he settled down by his nest and began to munch on the stinky fruit.

Tom looked at his watch. "We'll have to hurry," he

announced. The boys carefully placed their feet in the fresh dinosaur prints outside the rock face and stepped backward out of the bright sunshine of Dino World into the darkness of the smugglers' cave. They squeezed through the gap, dashed out of the cave, and burst out onto Smugglers' Point. Beneath them the waves were swirling close to the rocks.

"The beach will be cut off any minute," Tom said. "It's almost high tide."

They sprinted down the path and reached the beach just as the first gentle waves lapped at the bottom of the pathway.

"Just in time!" Jamie shouted, as they splashed through the shallow water and hurried to the other side of the cove.

"Ahoy there, me hearties!" Jamie's grandfather greeted them with a wave from the rocks beneath Sealight Head. "Are you ready for a crabbing adventure?"

"Just as long as there are no geysers or raptors," Tom whispered to Jamie as they scrambled up the rocks to join him.

Jamie grinned. "Ahoy there, Grandpa," he called. "We're always ready for a new adventure!"

Ahoy there, me hearties!

Far Away Mountains
Crashing Rock Falls
Great Plains
Fang Rock
Gingko Hill

GLOSSARY

Ankylosaurus — a vegetarian dinosaur known for its armored coat and clubbed tail. Its armor consisted of large bony bumps similar to the covering of modern-day crocodiles and lizards.

Fossil Finder — hand-held computer filled with dinosaur facts.

Geyser — a hot spring, heated by volcanic activity below the earth's surface, that erupts in a tall stream of hot water and steam from time to time.

Ginkgo — a tree native to China called a "living fossil" because fossils of it have been found dating back millions of years, yet they are still around today. Also known as the stink bomb tree because of its smelly apricot-like fruit.

Protoceratops — a horned, plant-eating dinosaur with a large head, neck frill, and parrot-like beak, roughly half the size of a triceratops.

Triceratops (T-Tops) — a three-horned, plant-eating dinosaur that looks like a rhinoceros.

Tyrannosaurus Rex (T-Rex) — a meat-eating dinosaur with a huge tail and two strong legs, but two tiny arms. T-Rex was one of the biggest, scariest dinosaurs.

Velociraptor — meat-eating dinosaur that was one of the smartest and fastest dinosaurs. Velociraptors were about the size of a turkey with a large, curved claw on both of their feet.

Wannanosaurus — a dinosaur that only ate plants and used its hard, flat skull to defend itself. Named after the place it was discovered: Wannano, in China.